For: Muriël, Myrthe, Merel, and Marnick

First published in Belgium and Holland by Clavis Uitgeverij, Hasselt – Amsterdam, 2012
Copyright © 2012, Clavis Uitgeverij

English translation from the Dutch by Clavis Publishing Inc. New York
Copyright © 2013 for the English language edition: Clavis Publishing Inc. New York

Visit us on the web at www.clavisbooks.com

Don't Be Afraid to Say No! written by Ilona Lammertink and illustrated by Lucie Georger
Original title: *Dan zeg ik toch gewoon nee!*
Translated from the Dutch by Clavis Publishing

ISBN 978-1-60537-148-1

This book was printed in April 2013 at Proost, Everdongenlaan 23, 2300 Turnhout, Belgium

First Edition
10 9 8 7 6 5 4 3 2 1

Clavis Publishing supports the First Amendment and celebrates the right to read

Bumps & Bubbles

Don't Be Afraid to Say No!

No!

Ilona Lammertink & Lucie Georger

Clavis

Everyone's busy at their desks. Everyone except Jill. She's gazing dreamily outside. She's excited for the dismissal bell to ring because after school, Susie's coming to her house to play. Susie's one of the nicest girls in class—she's almost never afraid and everyone wants to be her friend.

Briiing!

Finally! It's time to play!

Jill and Susie are playing in Jill's room.

"You've got so many stuffed animals," Susie says cheerfully. "Let's play zoo with them!" Jill agrees and they arrange all the stuffed animals on the floor. One by one, they care for each animal—picking them up, feeding them, making sure they're not sick, and then cuddling them. Just like real zookeepers!

"Who's that?" asks Susie, pointing to Hopper, the stuffed rabbit Jill just got for her birthday. Hopper has a ribbon around his neck with a little blue brush on it so you can comb his soft white fur. Hopper is Jill's very favorite stuffed animal.

Susie picks up Hopper. She starts to cuddle him and brush his fur.

Jill bites her lip. She wishes Susie wouldn't play with Hopper,

but she doesn't dare say so.

"He's so sweet," Susie says. "Can I borrow him overnight?"

Jill suddenly gets a weird tickly feeling in her stomach.

She doesn't want Susie to take Hopper home with her.

But if she says **no**, maybe Susie won't want to play with her anymore.

And that's why Jill says, "Yes."

The play date is over and Hopper disappears into Susie's backpack.

Susie's going home with Hopper and Jill's staying behind. Alone.

She's mad at herself. *I wish I had said "**No**."*

At school the next morning Jill runs up to Susie. "Did you bring Hopper with you?" she asks eagerly. Susie takes Hopper from her backpack. There's the little blue brush dangling from his neck, but...there are teeth marks on the handle! Someone's chewed on it!
"My dog wanted to play with Hopper, too," Susie says shyly. "Sorry."

Jills hugs Hopper. She turns around and walks away. Then she feels something sticky in Hopper's soft fur. It's like someone's spilled honey all over his tail! Jill's sad and a little mad.

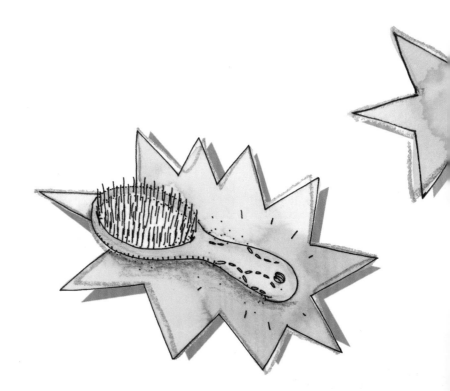

One night, Jill's parents are on a trip, so she's staying with her next-door neighbors. The boys next door, Tom and Kev, are a little older than Jill, but they all go to the same school. Tom and Kev want to watch a video that Jill hasn't heard of. The pictures on the box look like it's going to be really scary. Jill would rather watch the video with the dolphins on the box, but she doesn't dare say **no**....

Tom and Kev are laughing at the movie. They love watching the huge, angry monsters. The monsters scare Jill, but she doesn't want to say so. She just shuts her eyes.
*I wish I had said "**No**."*

That night, Jill has trouble falling asleep. All around her she sees those scary monsters! She thinks she can even hear their angry voices! Jill crawls further under the blankets and squeezes Hopper tightly. *If only I'd dared to say **No**!*

Jill's in the park with kids from the neighborhood. She looks over
at the tall clock tower. She's supposed to go home when the two hands
are almost standing together on the six.

"Look! A hot air balloon!" Bailey shouts. "It's flying so low—it's going to land
somewhere near us. Let's go see. You coming, Jill?"
Jill checks the big clock again. She should go home, but...she nods.
She knows her parents will be upset with her. *I wish I had said "**No**."*

Jill's crying in her room. Mom and Dad are mad because she's come home late. She wishes more than anything that she'd dared to say **no** to Bailey and the others.

Mom comes in and sits on the bed. "What happened, Jilly?" she asks gently.

Jill blurts out: "I don't ever say **no** to my friends because I'm scared they won't like me anymore and won't want to play with me! I just can't say **no**, even if they're doing things I don't like!"

Mom wipes away Jill's tears and hugs her. "Jill, honey, you can say **no**. You actually say **no** to your very best friend all the time."

"What do you mean?" Jill asks. "Who do I say **no** to?"

"Come with me." Mom takes Jill's hand.

Mom leads Jill to the big mirror in the corner.

"Take a good look in there," Mom says. "Every time you say **yes** to your friends, you're really saying **no** to the girl in the mirror!"

Susie, I want Hopper to stay here...

"I've really said **no** lots of times, haven't I?" Jill says to Mom. "To myself."

"That's right! You've practiced saying **no** over a thousand times without even realizing it. Real friends won't get upset if you say **no** every now and then," Mom explains.

"Sometimes, it's even brave to say **no**. Would you be angry if a friend said **no** to you?"

Jill smiles. "**No!**" she shouts.

Jill feels a lot better.

Saying **no** doesn't seem nearly so hard anymore.

"I'll just say **no** when...

I have to do something
I don't want to do.

I'm scared.

Information for parents and teachers

All toddlers learn to say no. Often called "the terrible twos," this phase most children go through of not listening well and being stubborn often frustrates parents and teachers. For the child, though, this period is critical to building self-confidence. The child discovers he or she can have their own opinion, and that saying no can mean a certain strength and power over a situation. By practicing saying no, the child explores the boundaries of his or her environment. Because not everything goes the way the child wants it to go, the child learns that saying no often triggers a reaction in another person and that's how the child begins to feel empathy, taking someone else into account.

Some children find it very hard to say no. Still, it's important every child learn that they can and should say no when they have to. This skill makes someone more stable and more confident. Children who can't say what they're really feeling, particularly in uncomfortable situations, are often more vulnerable. These children, unfortunately, are more often victim of bullies and other intimidators.

Self-confidence

How well a child can say no depends on his or her self-image: those who have a positive self-image generally have more overall self-confidence. Of course, elements such as character and family history play roles in a child's self-image, but a child will feel safer and will develop a positive self-image growing up in an environment where he or she can be him- or herself and where there's encouragement for personal growth and room to learn from one's 'mistakes.'

In the first years of a child's life, parents and teachers play an important role in building self-confidence in a child. As soon as children start going to school, the opinions of friends and peers will become the primary influencers of self-confidence. Children like to belong, to feel part of the group, and are prepared to cross lines to achieve this goal, even if that means going against what they really want or feel. The sooner a child learns to stand up for him- or herself and indicate their boundaries, the safer and stronger that child will be.

Increasing self-confidence

The basis for self-confidence is unconditional love, respect, and acknowledgement: let your child see that you love him or her. When a child feels that he or she is worthy, a positive self-image and healthier behaviors will come naturally. A compliment, a wink, a thumbs-up, a pat on the back, or a hug—even these small, simple gestures can and do make a child feel appreciated, respected, and acknowledged.

At the same time, offering constructive criticism to